The Mouse's Wedding

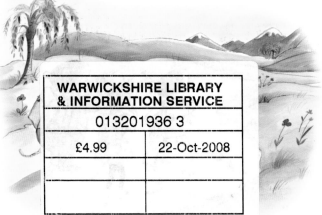

Retold by
Mairi Mackinnon

Illustrated by
Frank Endersby

Reading Consultant: Alison Kelly
Roehampton University

This story is about

Father
Mouse,

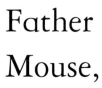
Mother
Mouse,

Miss
Mouse,

the sun,   a cloud,

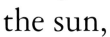

the wind,   a wall

and a handsome
young mouse.

Once there was a family
of mice – Father Mouse,

Mother Mouse and little
Miss Mouse.

And then one day
Miss Mouse wasn't so
little anymore.

"Goodness me!" said
Father Mouse. "It's time
you got married."

"Pack your bag," he said.
"We're going on a journey."

"We must find you the best, most powerful husband in the world!"

"Who could that be?"
asked Miss Mouse.

Father Mouse thought
for a moment. "The sun!"
he said.

"He makes our days
bright and warm, and
helps the flowers grow.
Let's ask him."

The mouse family climbed a high mountain.

They waited until
evening, when the sun
was low in the sky.

"Oh Mr. Sun," said Father Mouse. "You are more powerful than anyone else in the world..."

"Powerful? Me?" said
the sun. "Oh no, I don't
think so."

"Look at that cloud,"
said the sun.

"He can cover my face,
and block all my light
and warmth. There's
nothing I can do."

"Well, then, we must talk to the cloud," said Father Mouse.

The mouse family went
a little way down the
mountain and slept until
morning.

When they woke up, there
was the cloud resting on
the mountain top.

"Oh Mr. Cloud," said Father Mouse. "You are more powerful than anyone else in the world..."

...aren't you?

"Powerful? Me?" said the cloud. "Oh no, I don't think so."

"Wait until the wind blows," said the cloud.

"He can push me around, this way and that way. There's nothing I can do."

"Well, then, we must talk to the wind," said Father Mouse.

Mother Mouse gave
everyone some crumbs for
breakfast, and the mice
waited.

The wind soon rose and
blew the cloud away.

"Oh Mr. Wind," said Father Mouse. "You are more powerful than anyone else in the world..."

"Powerful? Me?" said the wind. "Oh no, I don't think so."

"Up here
I can blow
where I like,"
said the wind.
"But when I meet a wall,
there's nothing I can do."

"Well, then, we must talk to a wall," said Father Mouse.

Talk to a wall?

The mouse family set off
down the mountain.

After a while, they came to
a high wall.

"Oh Mr. Wall," said Father Mouse. "You are more powerful than anyone else in the world..."

"Powerful? Me?" said
the wall. "Oh no, I don't
think so."

"I may look strong and tall," said the wall, "but I can feel a little mouse, nibbling me to dust. There's nothing I can do."

34

"Well, then, we must
talk to the mouse," said
Father Mouse.

"Oh yes, please let's talk to the mouse," said Miss Mouse.

They made their way
along the wall. There
was a mousehole and a
handsome young mouse.

Miss Mouse smiled at him.

"Oh Mr. Mouse," said Father Mouse. "You are more powerful than anyone else in the world... aren't you?"

"Well..." the mouse began.

"You're more powerful than the wall," said Miss Mouse quickly.

"...who is more powerful than the wind," added Mother Mouse.